P9-CKX-247

Thanks to Lucy

Thanks to Lucy

by Ilene Cooper

illustrated by David Merrell

A STEPPING STONE BOOK™

Random House New York

With great thanks to my friends at Booklist, *past and present.*
It hardly ever seemed like work.
—I.C.

For Suzanne: I cannot thank you enough for the many years
of friendship and hard work.
—D.M.

Visit us on the Web!
SteppingStonesBooks.com
randomhouse.com/kids

Educators and librarians, for a variety of teaching tools, visit us at
RHTeachersLibrarians.com

Library of Congress Cataloging-in-Publication Data
Cooper, Ilene.
Thanks to Lucy / by Ilene Cooper ; illustrated by David Merrell. — First edition.
p. cm. — (Absolutely Lucy ; #6)
"A Stepping Stone book."
Summary: "Bobby Quinn has a lot to be thankful for this Thanksgiving—his grandmother's visit, an adopted baby brother or sister on the way—but what he's most thankful for is his beagle, Lucy, who hasn't been acting like herself lately."—Provided by publisher.
ISBN 978-0-375-86998-3 (pbk.) — ISBN 978-0-375-96998-0 (lib. bdg.) —
ISBN 978-0-375-98638-3 (ebook)
[1. Dogs—Fiction. 2. Beagle (Dog breed)—Fiction. 3. Thanksgiving Day—Fiction. 4. Babies—Fiction. 5. Adoption—Fiction. 6. Brothers and sisters—Fiction.]
I. Merrell, David, illustrator. II. Title.
PZ7.C7856Th 2013 [Fic]—dc23 2012041337

Printed in the United States of America
10 9 8 7 6 5 4 3 2 1
First Edition

Contents

Bagels and Beagles

CLANG! BANG!

Bobby Quinn sat up in bed. What was that noise? It was coming from the kitchen.

Bobby looked at his clock. It was early. Lucy, his little beagle, was asleep at the foot of his bed. Lucy was supposed to stay in her own bed. But most nights she climbed in with Bobby.

Lucy raised her head and gave a small

howl. The small howl turned into a big yawn. She snuggled back down on the blanket. Lucy liked to sleep in on the weekends, just like Bobby.

CRASH!

Bobby jumped out of bed. What in the world was happening downstairs?

In a flash, Lucy was on the floor and running right behind him.

When they got to the kitchen, Bobby's eyes grew wide. Usually when there was a mess in the house, it was because Lucy had gotten up to something or into something.

This mess looked like it was all his mom's fault.

A couple of cookie sheets were on the floor. So was a metal pie plate. A shiny lid, upside down, lay nearby.

"Mom, what's going on?" Bobby asked.

Mrs. Quinn's back was to him. "I'm trying to find the roaster," she mumbled.

"The rooster?" Bobby asked, confused.

"The roaster," she said, a little more loudly. "For the Thanksgiving turkey."

Then she pulled a few more pots and pans out of the overcrowded cabinets. Most of them fit on the counter and table, but a dented pan tumbled to the floor.

"Why haven't I cleaned out these cabinets?" Mrs. Quinn moaned. "I should have thrown away half this stuff."

Lucy began sniffing at the pie plate. She had a very good nose. Maybe she could still smell the apple pie Mrs. Quinn had made last week.

Bobby's father came in through the back door. He seemed as surprised as Bobby when he saw the pots and pans on the floor.

He looked at Lucy. No, Lucy couldn't have done all this.

"Jane," Mr. Quinn said, clearing his throat, "I take it you didn't find the roaster?"

Mrs. Quinn sat down on a kitchen chair. "No. I didn't find the roaster."

Bobby glanced at Lucy. She was now pushing a pot lid across the floor with her

paw. She seemed to think it was a new game.

Bobby got Lucy's kibble and poured some into her bowl. That would keep her busy. The last thing his mother needed was for Lucy to come up with a new, noisy game.

"There's just so much to do," Mrs. Quinn said. She threw up her hands. "Thanksgiving is almost here. We have company coming.

I have a project to finish at work. I haven't baked the pies yet. We've got to clean the whole house. And I don't know where the roaster is."

There was a tremble in Mrs. Quinn's voice.

Bobby and his father looked at each other. Uh-oh! Was Mom having a meltdown?

Mr. Quinn went to his wife and kissed her on the top of her head. "Don't worry, Jane. Bobby and I will help. We will make sure everything gets done."

"Absolutely," said Bobby. *Absolutely* was his favorite word. It meant FOR SURE in big capital letters.

Now his mother was smiling. "Thanks. I should have known I could count on my two guys."

"Lucy will help, too," Bobby said.

Lucy heard her name. She looked up

from her food and tilted her head. *How am I supposed to help?* she seemed to say.

"Lucy will help by staying out of trouble," Bobby said firmly.

Oh, that. Lucy went back to eating her food.

Bobby and his parents laughed.

"I know you'll keep an eye on her," Mrs. Quinn said. "And that's one less thing I have to worry about."

Mr. Quinn put a brown paper bag on the counter. He liked to get fresh-baked bagels on the weekend. Then he poured coffee. Bobby got out the milk. Mrs. Quinn cut the bagels and found the butter and jam in the refrigerator. They sat down to breakfast.

"Who exactly is coming for Thanksgiving?" Bobby asked.

Mrs. Quinn counted on her fingers. "The

three of us. Your aunt Kay and uncle John. Ryan and Brian. And, of course, Nanny Ann is coming in from Washington, D.C. Eight."

Eight didn't seem like that big of a number, but it would make for a full house. Bobby's aunt and uncle and cousins lived about an hour away. The families mostly got together for things like birthdays and holidays. His cousins Ryan and Brian were twelve, and they were twins. They usually didn't pay much attention to Bobby.

Nanny Ann was his mom's mother. His dad's parents lived in Florida. He wished he could see more of all of his grandparents.

Bobby took a sip of his milk. "Don't forget the Thanksgiving assembly. That's the day before Thanksgiving." He hoped his mother wouldn't think it was just one more thing she had to do.

But Mrs. Quinn was smiling. "Nanny and I will be coming to see you. She's looking forward to it."

Mr. Quinn buttered his second bagel. "Last time I heard, your class hadn't decided what you were going to do."

"We have to decide soon," Bobby said. "Mrs. Lee said she is tired of Pilgrims."

Bobby hoped he wouldn't have a speaking part in the third-grade program. Bobby was shy. Not as shy as he used to be. He could even give a report in front of the whole class now without whispering and getting red in the face.

Getting up on a stage, though? In front of half the school? That sounded awful.

Lucy was finished with her breakfast. She knew what came next. Time for her walk. She stood by Bobby's chair, and she looked at him with her big brown eyes.

Bobby got up. "Well, Lucy, since you asked so nice, let's go." He grabbed Lucy's leash from the hook by the door. Usually the leash made Lucy prance and howl. Today she sat quietly while Bobby hooked the leash to her collar.

Maybe, he thought, *keeping Lucy out of trouble isn't going to be so hard after all.*

Ideas

Bobby and the rest of Mrs. Lee's third-grade class pulled their chairs into a circle.

Mrs. Lee held her hand up. That meant *Quiet!*

"Class, we have just one week before the Thanksgiving assembly," Mrs. Lee said. She looked at her students sitting around her in the circle. "Let's put our heads together and come up with a program today."

Bobby watched his friends Shawn and Dexter giggle as they hit their heads together lightly.

Mrs. Lee frowned at them. "Boys, I need ideas, not goofing around."

Marta raised her hand.

"Yes, Marta?" Mrs. Lee asked.

"We could do a skit about the ways

Thanksgiving is celebrated in other countries," Marta said.

Mrs. Lee thought about that. "Well, there are harvest festivals in other countries. I don't think we have time to learn about them, though. But it was a good idea, Marta."

Candy, another friend of Bobby's, raised her hand.

Uh-oh, Bobby thought. *Candy's ideas can be doozies*.

"Yes, Candy?" Mrs. Lee nodded at her.

"I was thinking about the turkeys. The poor turkeys. We could do a play about the turkeys and how they gotta be worried when Thanksgiving rolls around. You know, they're happy in the summer. Not a care in the world. Then the leaves start falling. Pretty soon, it's going to be time—"

"You know, Candy," Mrs. Lee interrupted, "I'm glad you're thinking about the turkeys. But I'm not sure turkeys actually worry."

"Maybe they should," Candy muttered to herself.

Mrs. Lee sighed. "Anyone else?"

Jack raised his hand. "Thanksgiving is about being thankful."

Now Mrs. Lee was smiling. "That's exactly right. What did you have in mind?"

Jack looked embarrassed. "Well, nothing, really."

"All right, Jack has given us the start of a good idea," Mrs. Lee told the class. "Let's build on it. What kind of program can we do about giving thanks?"

"We could say things we're thankful for," Dexter said.

"Like what?" Mrs. Lee asked.

"I'm thankful for my grandmother's sweet potato pies," Dexter said. "And she makes two of them at Thanksgiving."

"I'm thankful that my dad got a job," a girl named Ally said.

"I'm thankful that medicine made my dog Butch's gas better. Not so stinky," Candy said.

Everybody burst into giggles at that. Even Mrs. Lee laughed.

"Well, we probably all have things we are thankful for. I know a good song about Thanksgiving. Why don't we all say what we are thankful for at our program and then sing?" Mrs. Lee suggested.

Most of the boys and girls nodded. They liked the idea.

Bobby didn't like Mrs. Lee's idea. Why couldn't they just sing the song and be done with it? Then he had an idea. He raised his hand.

"Yes, Bobby?" Mrs. Lee looked a little surprised. Bobby almost never asked questions in class.

"Maybe we could draw pictures," he said.

"Pictures?" Mrs. Lee repeated. She seemed puzzled.

"Draw pictures of the things we are thankful for." Bobby spoke softly. He wondered if Mrs. Lee even heard him.

Mrs. Lee thought about it for a moment. "That's a good idea, Bobby. We won't just tell the audience what we are thankful for. We can show them. We'll put our pictures on poster boards so the audience can see them. If you don't want to draw, you can cut pictures out of a magazine. Or blow up photographs." Mrs. Lee seemed pleased.

Bobby smiled. No magazine pictures for him. He liked to draw. He was good at drawing. And if he held up a poster, he could hide behind it.

When school was over, Bobby and Shawn walked home together. They lived across the street from each other.

"So, what are you going to draw for the Thanksgiving program?" Shawn asked Bobby.

"Lucy, of course," Bobby answered. "What about you?" Shawn liked to draw, too.

"I'm not sure," Shawn said. "Maybe Sara and Ben."

Bobby was surprised. Sara was Shawn's older sister. Ben was his younger brother. Sara could be bossy. Ben could be a pain.

Bobby said goodbye to Shawn. He wondered, would he want to draw his brother or sister if he had one? He might find out pretty soon. The Quinns were waiting for the adoption agency to bring them a baby. The agency had made sure the Quinns were a good family. The baby's room was almost ready. But there was no word on when a baby might arrive.

Bobby had lots of feelings about a new baby.

He was excited. A baby might be fun.

He was worried. What if his parents liked the baby more than him?

He was nervous. What would it really be like to have a baby in the house?

And the biggest feeling of all? It was nerves, mixed with worry, topped by excitement. What kind of big brother would he be?

Bobby thought about when Lucy had arrived. She was squirmy, squiggly, noisy, sometimes stinky. A baby would probably be all that. But Lucy was very sweet, too.

Could a baby be as sweet as Lucy?

Slowly Bobby walked into his house.

Usually Lucy greeted Bobby at the door with a couple of yelps, a few jumps, and a howl. Today she just rubbed her head against his leg.

"Hey, girl." Bobby patted her between the ears. "We'll go out for a walk in a minute. First I want to say hi to Mom."

Lucy trotted behind Bobby as he walked into the kitchen. His mother was on the phone.

"Yes . . . ," she said. "Yes, I understand. Yes, of course. Thank you, Mrs. Brady."

Bobby knew who Mrs. Brady was. He called her the Baby Lady. She was the social worker from the adoption agency.

Mrs. Quinn hung up the phone. She had a funny look on her face.

Bobby hoped this wasn't going to be the start of another meltdown.

Mrs. Quinn came over to Bobby and gave him a big hug. She was smiling, but she had tears in her eyes, too.

"Mom, what is it?" Bobby asked.

"It looks like we're going to get a baby!"

"We are? When?" Bobby asked.

"Mrs. Brady couldn't say exactly," his mother told him. "But she did say it would be soon."

Bobby gulped. Was he ready to be a big brother . . . *soon*?

3

Getting Ready

Bobby's parents had told him about the adoption a few months ago. Then it had seemed like something that might happen someday.

Someday was getting closer.

Bobby tried to pin down his parents at dinner. "How soon is soon?" he asked.

Mr. and Mrs. Quinn looked at each other. "A few months?" Mr. Quinn said.

Mrs. Quinn nodded. "We don't know exactly when the baby will be born."

"But it won't be before Thanksgiving?" Bobby asked.

Mrs. Quinn looked startled. "Oh, I don't think so."

"Well, the baby's room is almost ready," Mr. Quinn said. "The walls are painted. The curtains are up."

"Now you just have to put the crib together," Mrs. Quinn said.

Mr. Quinn cleared his throat and spent a long time buttering his bread. "Yes. I'll do that this weekend."

Bobby knew his dad had already tried to put the crib together. More than once. Last time he'd finished with two extra pieces.

"Harder than it looks," his father had muttered.

After dinner, Bobby decided to start his picture of Lucy for the Thanksgiving program. He got out his art supplies.

Bobby was very good at drawing people. Drawing animals was much harder. He knew from past experience that drawing horses was really, really hard.

He hoped beagles were easier.

Bobby settled himself in a comfortable chair in the living room.

"Lucy," he called.

Lucy knew her name. She pattered into the room.

"Lucy, I'm going to draw a picture of you," Bobby informed her. "Sit!"

Lucy sat. For about three seconds. Then she flopped down on the floor.

"Well, okay," Bobby said. "At least you're not jumping around."

He started drawing Lucy on his pad of paper. He got the shape of her head right. He added Lucy's long velvety ears. She looked up at him, and he drew her chocolate-colored brown eyes. Her nose was harder.

Should he try to draw her whole body? Bobby wondered. Maybe he should draw her all stretched out like she was right now. How long would Lucy stay like that?

To his surprise, Lucy stayed still. She twitched her tail back and forth. She panted a little. But Bobby was able to finish his sketch.

"Good girl!" Bobby told Lucy. He patted her head. She licked his hand.

Bobby looked at his drawing. It had come out better than he expected. Later he would paint Lucy's picture on poster board. He hoped that would turn out well, too.

The next day at school, Mrs. Lee asked

her students how the pictures were coming. Everybody started talking at once.

"I'm trying to draw our new house," said Marta. "I can't get the porch right at all."

"You think that's hard?" Jack said. "Try drawing hearing aids!" Jack had come to the school at Halloween time. Now that he had a new hearing aid, he could really be a part of Mrs. Lee's third-grade class.

Mrs. Lee said, "One at a time, please."

A few more kids talked about their pictures. Then Candy raised her hand and said, "My picture is a secret."

Bobby and Shawn looked at each other. Candy liked to talk. A lot. Could she really keep anything a secret?

After a few more children shared, Mrs. Lee said, "I have an idea. What if we wrote about what we're grateful for in rhyme?"

The class was silent. Rhyme?

Mrs. Lee must have read their minds. "I know. Putting thoughts down on paper is one thing. Making a short poem out of them is a little harder."

A lot harder, Bobby thought.

"But why don't we all give it a try?" Mrs. Lee said. "It might be fun." She added, "We can write our poems on the backs of the posters. That way they will be easier to read."

And hide behind, Bobby thought, perking up.

When the last bell rang and the kids were putting on their jackets, Bobby asked Candy, "So, what's your surprise?"

Candy pretended to zip her lip.

Shawn laughed. "You can't tell us anything about it?"

"Well . . ." Candy couldn't stay zipped for

long. "I'll tell you one thing. You and Bobby are a part of it."

Bobby and Shawn looked at each other.

"We are?" Bobby asked.

Candy grinned. "You'll find out soon enough."

My Pie

Bobby wandered into the kitchen. Lucy trotted right behind him.

Mrs. Quinn was making pies. She had flour on her hands and her apron. She had a dot of flour on her nose.

"Mom, what rhymes with *Lucy*?" Bobby asked.

"What do you think rhymes with *Lucy*?" his mother asked.

"All I could think of was *juicy,*" Bobby replied.

"Well, that's a start," Mrs. Quinn said. She rolled out the pie dough on a board covered in flour.

Bobby climbed on a stool next to the counter. "Not really. I have to come up with a poem about Lucy for the Thanksgiving poster. I can't say, 'Lucy is juicy.' "

Lucy, who was trying to climb onto Bobby's lap, started barking. She seemed to say, *Don't call me juicy.*

Bobby picked her up. Lucy drooled a bit as she made herself comfortable.

"I guess she can be a little juicy." Bobby picked up a napkin and rubbed at the wet spot on his pants. "But I don't want to say that in a poem."

"How about you come up with a rhyme

for *dog* instead?" Mrs. Quinn suggested.

"Dog, log, hog . . ." Bobby rattled off a few rhyming words. He didn't see what he could do with any of those.

Mrs. Quinn took a pie out of the oven. It smelled wonderful. Lucy lifted her nose and gave a long sniff.

"What kind?" Bobby asked.

"Apple," his mother answered. "This next one is pumpkin."

"Yay!" Bobby cheered. Pumpkin was his favorite.

Lucy smelled the apple pie. She wiggled a little in its direction.

"No, Lucy," Bobby said firmly, and held her tighter. "I guess *wiggly* is a word for Lucy."

He couldn't think of any words that rhymed with *wiggly,* though. Well, there

was *Wrigley.* Wrigley Field was where his favorite baseball team, the Chicago Cubs, played. But it didn't make much sense to say Lucy was wiggly and would like to visit Wrigley. Even if he wanted to take her, dogs weren't allowed in the ballpark.

The doorbell rang. Lucy jumped off Bobby's lap.

Bobby followed Lucy to the door. Through the glass on the side of the door, he saw Candy. Butch was with her. They both looked eager to get out of the cold.

Bobby opened the door wide. "C'mon in."

Lucy looked at Butch and gave a little growl. Butch lunged toward Lucy and he started sniffing her. Then Lucy sniffed back. They remembered they were friends.

"Well, hello," Mrs. Quinn said, coming out of the kitchen.

"Hello, Mrs. Q.," Candy said. "Are you baking?"

Mrs. Quinn nodded. "Pie."

"Pie?" Candy seemed disappointed. "I don't like pie much," she said. "I like cake. 'Cause it has frosting. So, of course, I like cupcakes, too. And cookies. My mom makes special cookies for me with frosting on top. Then they're almost like eating cake. Peanut-butter cookies with chocolate frosting. Maybe my name should be Cookie instead of Candy. But not Cake. Cake would be a stupid name."

Bobby wasn't sure what to say to that, but he had to agree. Cake would be a stupid name.

Candy asked Bobby, "You're not allergic to peanuts, are you?"

"Nope," Bobby answered.

"Good. I'll bring you some cookies next time my mom bakes them. They're scrumpdidilumptious."

Candy got a dreamy look on her face. It was clear she'd like one of those chocolate-frosted peanut-butter cookies right now!

Mrs. Quinn walked over to the living room desk and pulled out a large envelope. "I have something for you, Candy. Here you go."

Candy didn't seem at all surprised to be getting an envelope from Bobby's mother. But Bobby was very surprised.

"What's that?" he asked, pointing to the envelope.

Candy grinned. "Can't tell you."

Bobby remembered something. "Is this about the Thanksgiving program?" he asked.

Just like she had done at school, Candy zipped her lip.

Bobby wondered if he should be worried. Candy could get carried away sometimes.

He was just about to try to get Candy to unzip her lip when a chorus of barks came from the kitchen.

Mrs. Quinn dashed out of the living room

and into the kitchen. Candy and Bobby followed her.

The first thing they saw was Butch standing with his front paws on the counter. The apple pie was just about in reach. He stretched toward it. *Woof!*

His long pink tongue flipped back and forth. Pie! Soon!

The second thing they saw was Lucy dancing around Butch, bark, bark, barking. If barks were words, Lucy would be saying, *Get away from that pie!*

"Butch!" Candy, Bobby, and even Mrs. Quinn yelled the dog's name at the same time.

Butch acted as if he didn't hear them. His eyes were on the prize. Just one more swipe, and he would have a paw full of apple pie.

Lucy ran between Butch's legs and the

counter. Then she gave one of her long howls. *Hoooooooooowwl!*

Butch couldn't ignore that.

He looked down at Lucy. She gave a little growl.

Butch looked surprised.

Lucy growled again.

Butch forgot about the pie. He backed off. All four paws were down on the floor.

Bobby picked up Lucy. “Good dog!” he said.

Candy pulled on Butch’s collar. “Bad dog!” she said.

Mrs. Quinn grabbed the pie and took it

off the counter. She put it on a shelf so high, even she almost had trouble reaching it.

"I think we better go," Candy said. "Butch likes pie much more than I do."

Nobody argued with her.

Candy and Butch headed for the door. "Mrs. Q., thanks for the . . ." Candy slapped her hand over her mouth.

"You're welcome," Mrs. Quinn said.

As soon as they were gone, Bobby tried to find out what was in the envelope.

Mrs. Quinn zipped her lip.

Bobby laughed. He knew the envelope had something to do with the Thanksgiving program. He just hoped it wasn't something that would embarrass him. He couldn't worry about it, though. He still had to come up with a poem for his poster.

He followed his mother into the kitchen.

Suddenly it came to him.

"Mom, I've got a word for Lucy that's easy to rhyme."

"What's that, Bobby?" she asked.

"*Best!*" And best of all, it described Lucy perfectly.

5

Oh, Baby!

Mrs. Quinn walked into the living room. She had a list in her hand.

Bobby was sitting on the couch. He was working on his poem. He had finished the art earlier in the morning. It had turned out great!

The picture of Lucy filled up the poster. Everyone at the program would be able to see Lucy's brown-and-white spots. Her silky ears. Her chocolate-drop brown eyes.

Mr. Quinn was sitting next to Bobby. He was trying to find the football game he wanted to watch on TV.

Mrs. Quinn walked over to them. She shook her list.

Bobby and Mr. Quinn looked up.

"Ah, are you trying to tell us something, Jane?" Mr. Quinn asked his wife.

"Why, yes, I am," Mrs. Quinn said with a smile. "We have a lot to do today." She looked down at her list. "We have to buy a Thanksgiving tablecloth. Some orange and brown candles. We need to pick up at least two folding chairs. And I have a bunch of things to get at the grocery store."

"The grocery store?" Mr. Quinn asked. "Again?"

"Yes." Mrs. Quinn nodded. "And we will

probably have to go back to the store a few more times before Thanksgiving."

Mr. Quinn sighed. "I'm sure we will."

Bobby was glad there was nothing for him to do on his mother's list. Then his mother said, "And, Bobby, I'm going to need you to clean up the guest room. Nanny is going to sleep in your room, and you'll sleep in there."

The guest room was the smallest room in the house. It was even too small to be the baby's room. It should have been called the guest closet.

"And then, while your dad and I are out shopping, you can go over to play at Dexter's house."

"Dexter?" Bobby asked nervously. He liked Dexter, but he had never been to his house.

“Yes. Shawn and his family are away. The last time I saw Dexter’s mom, she asked if you could come over someday. Well, today would be perfect,” his mother said. “I already arranged it.” She was looking at her list again.

“Okay,” Bobby said. There didn’t seem to be much room for discussion.

Bobby figured he might as well start on the guest room. His mother brought him a cardboard box. He was throwing a few newspapers and magazines into it when Lucy padded in.

Bobby thought Lucy might want to tear up the papers. She liked that. But Lucy just nosed around the pile of papers and hopped on the bed. Then she curled up.

This isn’t like Lucy, Bobby thought. She had been very quiet since her run-in with

Butch yesterday. Saving the pie seemed to have tuckered her out.

Bobby stopped what he was doing. He sat down next to Lucy and patted her on the head.

"Are you okay, girl?" he asked.

Lucy raised her head and looked at him.

Bobby felt Lucy's head the way his mother did when he was sick. It seemed to be all right. He touched her nose. It was wet like always. Bobby still wasn't satisfied.

He went downstairs. "Mom," he said, "I don't think Lucy is feeling well."

"Why do you say that?" his mother asked.

"She's not acting like herself. She's resting a lot more. She's pretty quiet."

Mrs. Quinn was looking through her coupons, getting ready for the shopping trip. "She was fine yesterday when she kept Butch away from the pie."

Bobby shook his head. "I think that tired her out."

Mrs. Quinn glanced up at Bobby. "Well, we can't do anything about it today, Bobby. The vet isn't open on Sunday. I don't think this is an emergency."

"No, probably not an emergency," Bobby agreed softly.

"We have to get you over to Dexter's," Mrs. Quinn said. "Put on your jacket. We're going to leave in a few minutes."

Bobby went to say goodbye to Lucy. She was still resting on the bed. "Be good, girl," he told her.

Lucy yawned. She didn't look like she was going to cause any trouble.

Bobby was nervous when his parents dropped him off at Dexter's house. He was fine going to Shawn's, but this was something new.

He took a deep breath while he was waiting for the door to open. Then he had a thought. His mom and Dexter's mom had arranged this playdate. Maybe Dexter didn't even want him to come over.

But there was a big smile on Dexter's face when he opened the door.

"Guess what? I've got a new set of Star Wars Legos!" Dexter exclaimed before Bobby could even say hello.

"Cool!" Bobby said.

"We can do a whole battle thing," Dexter told him, leading him up to his room.

Dexter's house was smaller than Bobby's, but more people lived there. Bobby was surprised that Dexter shared his room with his baby brother. That meant the room had a bed and a crib. A shelf for games sat below a shelf for stuffed animals.

Dexter pulled out the Legos. Bobby started looking at the pieces, but he was curious about the baby.

"How old is your brother?" he asked.

"Cam is almost a year old," Dexter said.

He plopped down on the floor and Bobby sat next to him.

"What's it like? Having a baby in the house, I mean?"

Dexter shrugged. "Okay, I guess. He's a baby, ya know?"

Bobby didn't know. But he guessed he would find out soon enough.

The boys were getting ready for a Star Wars battle when Dexter's oldest sister walked into the room. Cam was in her arms, and he was crying. Loudly.

"Hey, Ashley," Dexter said. "What's wrong with the little man?"

"He needs his diaper changed," Ashley told him.

Bobby tried to remember if he had ever seen a baby's diaper changed. If he had, he hadn't paid much attention.

"Well, who wants to help me?" Ashley asked.

Bobby was startled. She didn't mean him, did she?

But Dexter shook his head and said, "I've already done it twice today, Ashley." He pointed at Bobby. "Bobby can do it."

"Me? I don't know how," Bobby squeaked.

"You don't have to do much," Ashley said. "Just make sure he doesn't roll off the table."

"Roll off the table?" Bobby repeated.

Ashley motioned Bobby over to the small changing table in the corner of the room. She didn't seem like she would take no for an answer.

"Stand on this side of the table and hold on to his shoulder," Ashley ordered. "I'll change him from this side. Make sure he stays steady while I clean him up."

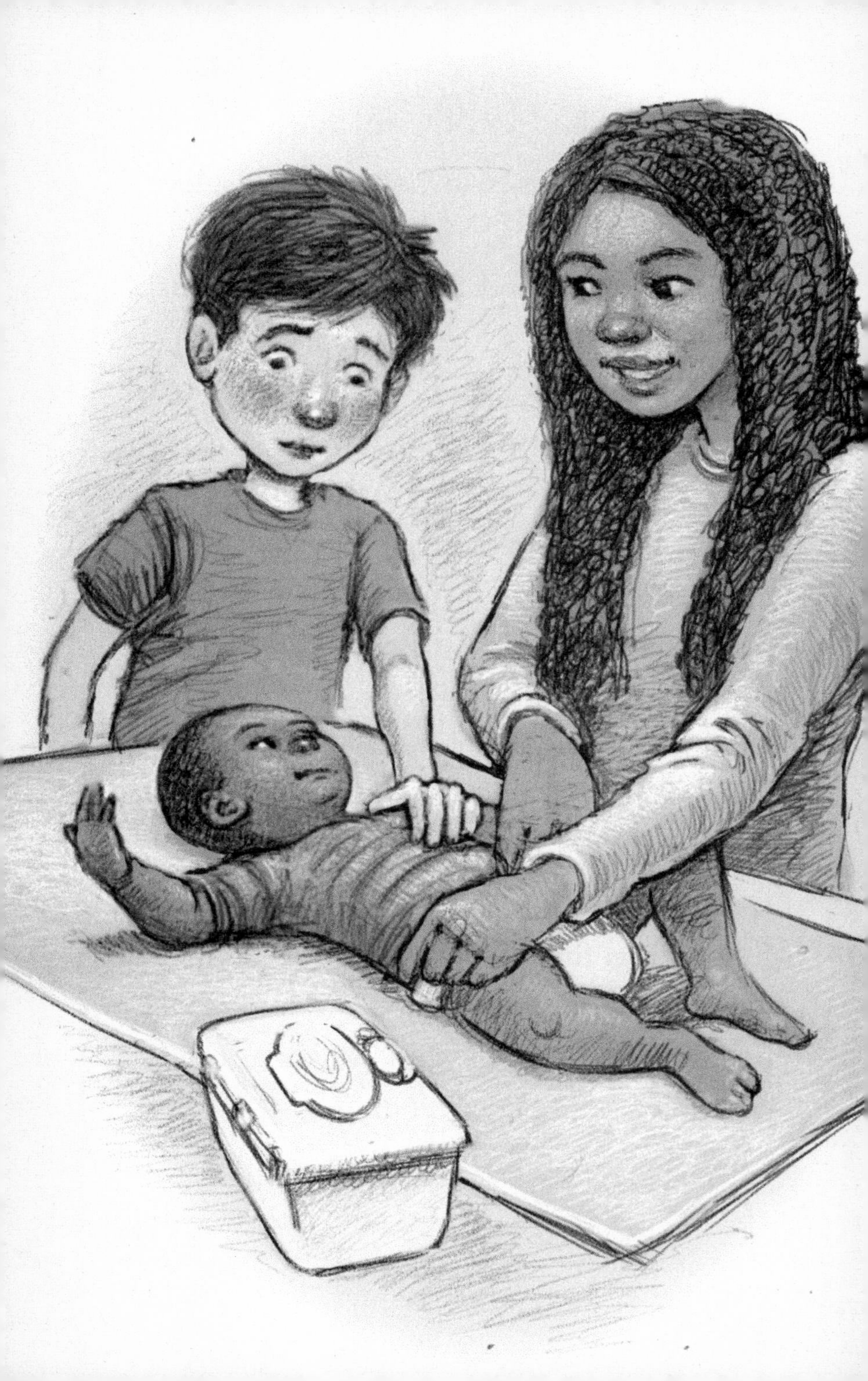

To Bobby, it sounded like a battle plan worthy of Star Wars.

Cam was still sniffling a little when Ashley carefully laid him down on the table. His big brown eyes kind of reminded Bobby of Lucy's.

Bobby held on to Cam's shoulder. Not too tightly, he hoped. But not too loosely, either.

Ashley acted as if she had changed a lot of diapers. So maybe she wasn't surprised by what was inside. But only one word came to Bobby's mind: *GROSS!*

It was a good thing Cam had gotten quiet. Crying, along with this mess, might have been more than Bobby could handle.

"The first time is always the worst," said Ashley. She quickly wiped Cam down, threw the dirty diaper in a bin, and wrapped Cam's bottom with a fresh one.

Bobby finally stopped holding his breath.

When she was done, Ashley helped Cam sit up. "Is that better, Cammie?"

Cam stuck his thumb in his mouth. He looked over at Bobby, and with his other hand, he hit Bobby on the nose. Then he took his thumb out and giggled.

It wasn't a hard slap. Cam wasn't even one, after all. Still, it was the first time Bobby could remember ever being touched by a baby. Was that what being a brother was all about? Slaps, giggles, and dirty old diapers?

Bobby wasn't sure how he felt about that. He wasn't sure at all.

6

Posters and Poems

Bobby lay in bed, looking up at the ceiling. He was wide-awake. Lucy was at his feet. Soft little snores meant that she was sleeping.

Spending the afternoon with Cam had made Bobby think. He didn't know if he was up for the job of big brother.

After Cam had been changed, he'd crawled around on the floor. Dexter and

Bobby had made sure that Cam didn't put any of the Star Wars pieces in his mouth. And there were lots of pieces!

When Cam was thirsty, Dexter gave him his water bottle.

When Cam started crying, Dexter found his favorite teddy bear under the bed.

Could Bobby do all that?

When Bobby finally fell asleep, he dreamed about babies.

The next morning, Bobby was sort of happy he had to go to school. There was too much going on at his house.

As Bobby searched for his book bag, his mother looked at her watch. "I have to pick up Nanny at the airport in a couple of hours. But before that I have to stop at work for a few things. Then once Nanny and I get back, we have to—"

Before his mother could finish, Bobby said, "And don't forget we have to take Lucy to the vet."

"Lucy?" Mrs. Quinn seemed like she didn't remember what Bobby was talking about. Then she said, "Oh, the vet."

Bobby pointed at Lucy's dish. It was still half full of kibble. "She's not eating much."

"I see," Mrs. Quinn said. "All right, we'll try to get Lucy there this afternoon."

Bobby wasn't sure that he liked the word *try.* He just knew Lucy wasn't feeling her best. He would make sure that Lucy made it to the vet later.

The school day went slowly. The class wasn't going to practice with their posters until the end of the day. Mrs. Lee kept the posters all together, leaning against the side of her desk. Bobby wished he had a chance to look at Candy's poster. He didn't really like surprises.

Finally it was poster time. Mrs. Lee had the kids line up at the back of the room.

"Okay, I know it's going to be cozy," Mrs. Lee said.

Cozy was Mrs. Lee's word for being right on top of each other. She handed out the posters.

"So no pushing or jabbing or even talking!" she went on. "We'll sing the song. Then when I point to you, step in front of the group and read your poem."

Shawn went first. On his poster, he had drawn his parents, his sister, Sara, and his brother, Ben. Shawn was in the picture, too. His mouse, Twitch, was on his shoulder.

Shawn was good at drawing. His poem was pretty good, too.

"I'm thankful for my family, my sister and
brother, Sara and Ben.
Someday Ben won't be a pest, but I'm not
sure when.
I also have a mouse named Twitch.
I'm thankful he doesn't make me itch."

A few more kids read their poems. One girl was thankful for books. A couple of boys were thankful for sports.

Then it was Candy's turn. Bobby was shocked when he looked at her poster. He glanced at Shawn. Shawn looked pretty surprised, too.

Bobby had thought maybe his mother had given Candy a picture of him. What he hadn't thought was that she would blow the picture up. Half the poster was taken up with Bobby's head. It was huge! The other half was Shawn, but at least it was a photo of his whole body. He didn't look like a giant head on a poster.

Candy stepped in front of the class.

"I'm thankful for my two great friends.

One is Bobby. One is Shawn.

They're lots of fun and never make me
yawn.
They used to be shy, but they're not
anymore.
Even when they were, they didn't make
me snore.
They're two friends I'll always keep.
They're so interesting, it's hard to sleep.
But if I do fall asleep—"

Mrs. Lee tried to interrupt. "Candy . . ."

Candy didn't seem to hear her. "I'm sure they'd wake me up—"

"Candy!" Mrs. Lee said a little more loudly.

Candy looked up. "Yes?"

"That's a very nice poem about Shawn and Bobby," she said.

Everyone was looking at either Shawn or

Bobby. Bobby could feel his face growing red.

"However," Mrs. Lee added, "all the poems have to be around the same length. So why don't you end with 'it's hard to sleep'?"

"Really?" Candy said, surprised. "Because I've got . . ." She counted the lines on the back of her poster board. "I've got eight more lines. And they rhyme."

"I'm sure they do," Mrs. Lee said. "But I'm afraid you'll have to stop where I told you."

Candy stepped back into the group. "Don't worry," she whispered loudly to Bobby and Shawn. "I'll read the whole thing to you later."

Bobby nodded.

Finally it was his turn to stand in front of his classmates. He could see they liked his picture of Lucy. A few of them pointed and there were lots of smiles.

"Lucy, my beagle, is the best.
You could search north, east, or west,
And you'd see she's better than the rest.
She's smart and friendly as can be.
I'm thankful she belongs to me."

"Very nice, Bobby," Mrs. Lee said. "Both the art and the poem will make the audience feel like they know Lucy."

"Thank you," Bobby said softly. He was glad that everyone would get to know how great Lucy was. But mostly, like the poem said, he was thankful she belonged to him.

7

Nanny and Lucy

"Bobby!" Nanny Ann reached for Bobby to give him a big hug when he got home.

Bobby felt shy. That seemed funny. Nanny was his grandmother, after all. But he didn't know her very well.

Bobby and his family had visited Nanny twice. Washington was very cool. It was the capital of the United States. There was a lot to see there. They had even visited the

White House, where the president and his family lived.

This was also the third time Nanny had visited them. Sometimes he talked to his grandmother on the phone or on the computer. That wasn't the same as giving her a hug.

He walked into her arms anyway. The hug felt pretty good.

Bobby pulled away and Nanny gave him a long look. "How are you, my boy?"

"Fine," Bobby said.

"I've met your dog, Lucy," Nanny said. "She's a sweet little thing."

Bobby was surprised to hear Nanny say that. Usually when new people came to the house, Lucy went, well, a little crazy. She would bark, jump on them, and maybe even chew their gloves. She had done that to Mrs.

Brady, the lady from the adoption agency.

Bobby was pretty sure that Nanny was the first person to describe Lucy as "a sweet little thing."

Bobby looked around for Lucy. "Uh, sometimes she can be pretty wild."

"Well, not today," Nanny said. She led Bobby over to the couch in the living room. "So sit down and tell me what's new."

Bobby didn't know where to start. He hadn't talked to Nanny in a while. Probably everything was new.

"I guess you know we're getting a baby," he began.

"I do!" Nanny said with a big smile. "I bet you're excited."

Bobby nodded. But not very excitedly.

"No?" Nanny asked.

Bobby shrugged.

Nanny ran her hand through Bobby's hair. "Getting a new baby is a big thing," she said.

"Yes. It is," Bobby agreed.

"Are you worried that the baby is going to take up too much of your parents' time?" Nanny asked.

Bobby shook his head.

"Oh," Nanny said. "Do you think the baby will be noisy, crying too much?"

"I know it will probably cry a lot. Babies do that," Bobby answered.

"Then what is worrying you?" Nanny asked.

Bobby looked at his grandmother. He didn't know her very well. But he felt like she knew him. From the look on her face, Bobby could tell she really wanted to help him.

He fiddled with a button on his shirt.

"I . . . well, I'm not sure I'll make a very good big brother."

Nanny looked surprised. "Oh, Bobby. I don't think that's true."

"Could be," Bobby replied.

Before Bobby could tell her more, his mother came bursting into the room.

"The adoption agency just called," Mrs. Quinn said in a voice that didn't sound quite like hers. She had a funny look on her face, too.

"Is the baby here?" Nanny and Bobby asked, almost at the same time.

"I don't know. Mrs. Brady just said she wants to see us right away. It will take a while to drive over to the agency. David is leaving his office now, and he's going to pick me up. I don't know what time we'll be back." Mrs. Quinn's words came out in a rush.

"That's all right," Nanny said. "I'm here. Bobby and I will take care of everything. Won't we, Bobby?"

"Sure," he said. He wasn't paying much attention, though. He could feel his stomach fluttering. Fluttering? Rolling! When his parents came back, would they have a baby with them?

Mrs. Quinn had barely had time to get her coat on when Bobby heard his father honking outside. She gave her mother a hug and Bobby a big kiss before she dashed out the door.

"I'll let you know what's happening just as soon as I can," she said.

Bobby and his grandmother looked at each other.

"Wow," Nanny said.

"Yeah. Wow," Bobby agreed.

"Everything's ready?" Nanny said. "The room, all the baby things?"

Bobby nodded. Everything was ready. Was he?

Just then, Lucy wandered into the room. She barked when she saw Bobby. She hopped on the couch and put her head in his lap.

She looked up at him with her big brown eyes. She looked over at Nanny.

"Her training seems to have worked. Is she always so calm now?" Nanny asked.

"No! No she isn't," Bobby answered.

What was the opposite of calm? Energetic? Wild? Crazy, even?

Suddenly something became very clear to Bobby. Lucy wasn't feeling well, and he knew what he had to do. He had to get Lucy to the vet. Now.

"Nanny," Bobby said, talking fast, "Lucy likes to run around. She likes to jump on people. She likes to howl. She's been too quiet for the last couple of days. Mom said she would get Lucy to the vet, but she's been so busy."

Nanny patted Lucy's head. "Well, she certainly doesn't seem like the Lucy you and your mom told me about."

Bobby felt hopeful. "So will you help me take her to the vet? Today?"

"Today?" Nanny seemed surprised. "I don't know about that."

"But, Nanny—" Bobby began.

"I don't know where the vet is. And it's getting late. The vet might not be able to see us."

Bobby didn't want to argue with his grandmother. He wasn't even sure what he should say. But when he looked at Lucy, all stretched out and tired, he knew he had to do something.

Bobby took a deep breath. "Nanny, *please.* I know Lucy isn't feeling well."

Nanny ran her hands through her wavy, short hair. She looked at Bobby. She looked at Lucy. Then she looked at Bobby again.

"All right, Bobby," she said. "You know Lucy best. Find the vet's number, and I'll see if he can get her in this afternoon. Then I'll text your parents and tell them what's up."

The next half hour was a rush. Lucy's vet, Dr. DiMarco, said he could fit them in if they could get there soon. Bobby had to wipe down Lucy's carrier and put her inside. Usually she didn't like it, but today she went inside without a peep. Then Bobby had to find his mother's spare car keys.

Nanny had a little trouble getting the car started.

"You know how to drive, right?" Bobby asked worriedly.

"Well, I don't have a car in Washington. I use the buses and the train. But I can drive."

When the car started, it jerked a bit. "How far is it to the vet's office?" Nanny asked.

"Just past downtown." Bobby pointed the way.

Nanny looked glad to hear it. They arrived at Dr. DiMarco's without any problems.

Lucy could tell she was someplace new. Bobby heard sniffing inside the carrier. She pushed her nose against the screen.

Nanny checked in at the front desk, and they were called into the examination room almost right away. Bobby let Lucy out of the carrier. Lucy sniffed and sniffed every part of the room. *Where was she? What was she doing here?*

Dr. DiMarco picked Lucy up and put her on the table. "Hi, Lucy." He patted her head. "What's going on with her?" he asked Nanny.

Nanny looked at Bobby. "I'm just visiting. Why don't you tell the doctor, Bobby?"

Bobby felt more shy than he had in a long time. He'd only met Dr. DiMarco once before, when Lucy first came to live with the Quinns. Dr. DiMarco was very tall and very serious. Bobby really didn't want to be the one to explain about Lucy, but he knew he had to do it. He was Lucy's owner, after all.

"Lucy usually likes to run around," he began slowly. "And sometimes she acts wild.

And she barks and howls. Lately she's been quiet and she seems tired. She sleeps more."

Bobby let out a breath. There, he had done it.

Dr. DiMarco nodded. "That was very helpful, Bobby. I know what to look for now."

The doctor checked Lucy's eyes. He lifted her floppy ears and examined them. He listened to her breathe. He poked her and prodded her. Lucy looked more surprised than anything. *Who was this man?*

When Dr. DiMarco finished, he picked

Lucy up in his arms. "Well, Bobby, I'm glad you were paying attention. I'm going to do some blood work on Lucy, but I think I know what is wrong with her. I think she has an infection."

"An infection?" Nanny repeated. "Is it serious?"

Bobby was glad Nanny had asked the question. Just thinking about Lucy being sick made him nervous.

"It can be. So it's a good thing you brought Lucy in when you did. The office is closing for the Thanksgiving holiday. We would have had to wait to treat Lucy until next week," Dr. DiMarco told them. "Now I can give Lucy a shot and some medicine, and I think before long, Lucy will be fine."

Bobby and Nanny looked at each other and smiled. Lucy was going to be all right!

Lucy slept on the way home. Bobby could hear her snores. Going to the vet had knocked her out.

As they pulled into the driveway, Nanny said to Bobby, "Well, I think you don't have to worry about whether you are going to be a good big brother anymore, Bobby."

Bobby was puzzled. "Why not?"

Nanny smiled at him. "You take such good care of Lucy. No matter what anybody said, you were going to make sure Lucy got to the vet. And you did!"

Nanny's words made Bobby feel good. Actually they made him feel great!

"That's what being a good brother is," Nanny went on. "Watching out for your brother or sister and making sure that they are okay. I can see you know how to do just that."

Bobby was about to say thank you when Nanny's cell phone rang.

She looked at the name. "It's your mom," she said.

Bobby watched as Nanny talked to his mother. Her face went from excited to surprised to more surprised. She kept repeating the word *two.*

"Is the baby here?" Bobby asked when she hung up.

Nanny looked as if she was trying to gather her thoughts. "It's a little more complicated than that, Bobby," she told him. "The adoption agency wants to know if your family will take twins."

"Twins?" Bobby repeated. No wonder Nanny kept saying the word *two*!

8

Twins

Bobby and his grandmother must have said the word *twins* ten times while they were waiting for his mom and dad to come home.

Now Bobby and Nanny were sitting around the dining room table with his parents, eating pizza, and talking about the babies.

"The babies are going to be born in a few weeks," Mrs. Quinn said, rubbing her forehead. “Mrs. Brady said she knows that we were only expecting one baby. We could wait and let the twins go to another home. This is a big decision.”

“Twins,” Nanny murmured again. “The baby’s room is only set up for one.”

Mr. and Mrs. Quinn looked at each other. Then they looked at Bobby.

“What?” he asked.

“Your room is bigger than the baby’s room,” his father said.

“The only room we can fit two cribs in is yours,” his mother added.

Bobby didn’t know what to say. It was hard enough to get his mind around two babies in the house. Now he would be trading rooms with them?

Nanny came to his rescue. “We don’t have to think about rooms right now. First you have to decide what you're going to do."

"You're right," Mrs. Quinn said. She put her slice of pizza down on the plate. She hadn't really eaten any of it. She just kept picking up the same slice and putting it back down.

"Ryan and Brian are twins," Bobby pointed out. "They'll be here for Thanksgiving. Let's just ask Aunt Kay and Uncle John if it's hard to raise twins."

All the adults laughed at that.

His father ruffled Bobby's hair. "I already know those boys are a handful. We've watched them grow up."

Bobby had another thought. He looked from his mother to his father. "Sometimes when parents are having a baby, they expect one but they get two, right?"

Mrs. Quinn nodded. "Yes, parents find

out along the way that they are having twins. They don't always know at the beginning."

"So they're surprised, just like we are?" Bobby asked.

His parents looked at each other for a moment. "You know, Bobby, you're exactly right," his father said slowly.

"Parents take what comes," his mother agreed. She smiled, really smiled, for the first time since she had gotten home.

"And what has come to us are two babies," Mr. Quinn laughed. "How do you feel about that, Jane?" he asked his wife.

Mrs. Quinn's smile turned into a laugh, too. "Great! We're having twins!" she agreed. "Bobby, you're so smart!"

"I am?" Bobby asked.

"You know how to ask the right questions," Nanny said.

Bobby was glad his questions had led to his mom and dad wanting twins. He was glad that everyone was smiling. "Hey, there's one important question I forgot," he said.

"What's that?" his dad wanted to know.

"Are the babies boys or girls? Or one of each?" Bobby couldn't believe he had gone this long without asking that.

"Girls!" his parents both said loudly.

Lucy came wandering into the dining room. Usually when someone said *girl* in a loud voice they were talking to her.

From the way she padded into the room, Bobby could see Lucy was feeling better. She had a spring in her step that had been missing. Her eyes looked brighter, too, as she put her paws up on Bobby's knees. *What's going on here?* she seemed to say.

Bobby picked Lucy up and put her on

his lap. She wiggled a little, but then she snuggled close to his chest.

"Lucy's feeling better," Bobby said. "Dr. DiMarco's shot must be working."

"You went to see Dr. DiMarco?" Mrs. Quinn asked, surprised.

"I texted you, Jane," Nanny said.

"We were so busy, I never checked my phone," Mrs. Quinn admitted. "What happened?"

Nanny, with Bobby chiming in, told the story of Lucy's visit to the vet.

"Oh, Bobby, I'm so sorry," his mother said. "I knew you wanted to get Lucy to the vet." She leaned over and rubbed Lucy's head.

"Well, Bobby knew what to do," Nanny informed them. "He found Dr. DiMarco's number, he cleaned off the carrier, he got the car keys, and he pointed me in the direction of the office."

"You sure take good care of Lucy," his father told Bobby. "Your new little sisters are lucky to have you as a big brother."

Sisters. Two baby sisters. Bobby felt a little like his head might explode. He hugged Lucy tighter. This must be how his parents were feeling right about now. There was so much to think about!

After Bobby got ready for bed, he peeked into the babies' room. Well, now his room, he guessed. It was smaller than his, but not too much smaller. But the paint! The room was a bright yellow. And those polka-dot curtains. They might as well have the word *baby* printed all over them.

Lucy skipped impatiently around Bobby as he stood in the doorway. *Let's go in,* she seemed to say. *Or go back to our room. But let's not just stand here. Hoooowl!* she added.

Now Bobby knew that Lucy was feeling better.

Bobby's mother heard the howl and came out of her bedroom. She saw Bobby looking at the yellow room. "Don't worry, Bobby," his mom told him. "We'll paint it. You can pick any color you want. And we'll move the curtains into your old room."

Bobby nodded. It was a start.

"And I'm thinking you'll need bunk beds," his mother went on.

"Bunk beds?"

"You might want to invite your friends over for sleepovers," Mrs. Quinn said.

Bobby thought about what his mother said while he was trying to fall asleep. Sleep

wasn't coming easy tonight. Not with so many things to think about. What a day!

He had tossed while remembering the vet visit. He had turned while wondering what it would be like when the babies arrived.

Now his thoughts were on the bunk beds.

He could see having Shawn sleep over at his house. He could see Dexter sleeping over, too.

It had only been last summer when he hadn't had any friends at all. Tonight he was planning sleepovers. And for his whole life he had been an only child. Now he was going to have sisters.

Things sure did change.

Lucy was in her own bed on the floor. Bobby's constant turning and twisting had bugged her. He had messed up the covers.

There wasn't a smooth spot for her to lie down.

But suddenly she jumped up on his bed and began licking his ear.

Bobby laughed. "Quit it, Lucy. It tickles!"

Lucy kept right on licking. It was like she was saying, *Last summer you weren't a dog owner. But you sure are now!*

Thanks for Everything!

Bobby stood on the stage of the auditorium. He could feel himself shaking a little. In the audience, his mother sat next to his grandmother. They were smiling at him. He tried to smile back.

He was glad he had his poster board of Lucy to cling to. The words of his poem were written in large letters on the back.

Bobby had figured he'd be nervous in the

days before the program, but too much had been going on to have time for nerves.

His parents were rushing around buying extra baby things.

His grandmother was cleaning the house and calling Aunt Kay to discuss food because his mom didn't have time to cook anything else.

Lucy was feeling better, which meant she was in the middle of everything. Every time a piece of furniture was moved, Lucy followed along to make sure it went into the right place. Every time a new item was brought into the house, Lucy wanted to sniff it. And maybe even give it a lick—or a chew if no one was watching.

Bobby had his hands full making sure that Lucy wasn't underfoot or in the way or causing trouble. He had to admit, though, he didn't mind Lucy causing a little trouble. That meant the old Lucy was back!

All the hubbub had made it easy to forget he was about to stand up in front of a huge room packed full of people. Now, though, here he was. Pretty soon, after the Thanksgiving song was over, it was going to be time to read his poem.

What no one knew was that he had changed the poem. Just two lines, but his scare about Lucy being sick made him want to say them.

With Mrs. Lee standing in front of them, the third grade sang their song. Then, one by one, the students stepped forward to say what they were thankful for.

Bobby watched as Dexter, Shawn, and Candy took their turns. The closer it came to his, the faster his heart beat. Finally Mrs.

Lee pointed at him. He tried to remember to speak up, just like she had told him to.

"Lucy, my beagle, is the best.
You could search north, east, or west,
And you'd see she's better than the rest.
Lucy was sick, but now she's fine.
I'm so thankful that she's mine."

Bobby hoped he hadn't talked too fast. When he looked out in the audience, though, his mother gave him a big thumbs-up.

Whew! He was thankful that was over.

The next morning, Bobby woke to good smells from the kitchen. Lucy was already downstairs, practically swooning from all the delicious odors. She stood in front of the oven panting, her tongue hanging out.

"There's not going to be any turkey for you, Lucy," Mrs. Quinn said. "It's not good for dogs."

Lucy didn't take her eyes off the stove where the turkey was roasting. She seemed to have a different idea.

"Bobby," his mother went on, "we're going to need your help today."

"Okay, what should I do?" he asked.

"You're on Nanny's team," his father said, coming in from the babies' room. "I'm working on the cribs, your mom is putting things away, and you're going to do whatever Nanny needs you to do for the dinner."

"And right now, I'd like you to set the table," Nanny said.

Bobby didn't like setting the table. It was hard to remember which was closer to the plate, the knife or the spoon. And now there were salad forks to worry about. He guessed his mom and dad had a lot more to worry about, though.

"What time are Aunt Kay and Uncle John coming?" Bobby asked.

"In a couple of hours," his mother said.

Never had a couple of hours flown by faster. After Bobby finished with the table, he dusted the living room and helped his grandmother put flowers in vases. The turkey came out of the oven, and Bobby gave Lucy a can of dog food to get her mind off the great smells.

Meanwhile, his mother made the house look neater and his father even managed to finish both cribs. "Once I figured out the first, the second one was easy," he said with a laugh.

"Their car is pulling into the driveway," Bobby said, looking out the window.

In a few minutes, the house was filled with aunts, uncles, cousins, noise, laughter, and, of course, barking.

"Lucy's not used to a crowd," Bobby's mother said, trying to pull her off Uncle John.

"She's adorable," he said, picking her up,

but Lucy wriggled right out of his arms and started pawing at Ryan's knees.

"You've gotten bigger since I saw you in July, Lucy," Ryan told her.

"A little bigger," Brian said. "She's still pretty small."

Lucy started barking. She barked loud. Lucy made up in noise what she might have lacked in size.

Aunt Kay was Mr. Quinn's sister, so she and her family weren't related to Nanny. But Nanny gave them all big hugs anyway.

"Hey, I hear you're adopting twins," Ryan said to Bobby's family.

"Too bad they're girls," Brian added.

"Aunt Jane, twins are double trouble," Ryan happily told Bobby's mother.

"Oh yeah, you're going to have your hands full," Brian said. "Just ask our mom."

"Well, we think two girls are going to be twice as nice," Mrs. Quinn said.

Bobby noticed that Brian and Ryan didn't answer that.

Lucy might not have been used to crowds, but they sure made her excited.

"Mom." Bobby pulled his mom aside. "I think I'd better take Lucy out."

Mrs. Quinn glanced at Lucy running in circles around Brian. "Good idea. Not too long, though. We'll be eating soon. Just long enough to get the wiggles out."

Well, that could be a while, Bobby thought. He put his jacket on, got Lucy's leash, and told his grandmother he would be right back.

Bobby and Lucy slipped out the door. Snow was just starting to stick on the ground, but flakes were swirling all around them.

Bobby looked up into the sky. The snowflakes were fun to watch. Lucy thought so, too. She didn't bark at them, though. She watched as they shimmered down and landed on her head and nose.

"Hey, girl, this is the first time you ever saw snow, right?" Bobby said.

Lucy just kept watching the snowflakes.

Bobby thought of all the things the babies would be seeing for the first time. Yes, there were going to be changes, but lots of fun might come with those changes.

Lucy batted her paws at a couple of big snowflakes. She gave one of her long Lucy howls.

She looked pretty pleased with herself when she was done.

"Not everything's going to change, though," Bobby said out loud. "You'll always be Lucy."

Lucy turned around to look at Bobby. She shook the snow off herself. She pulled on her leash. She was ready to walk now. Ready to run through the snow for the first time. She couldn't wait.

"Yep," Bobby said, following her lead, "you'll always be Lucy!"

Read more books about Bobby and Lucy!

Absolutely Lucy

Bobby's mother smiled. "Now it's time for your special present," she said.

His father said, "Close your eyes."

Bobby was glad to close his eyes. It would be easier to look surprised when he opened them.

"Okay, Bobby," his father called, "you can look!"

Bobby opened his eyes. He didn't have to pretend to be surprised. Or happy. In his father's arms was a puppy. The cutest, squirmiest little dog Bobby had ever seen.

Lucy on the Loose

"Ben!" Shawn said. "What happened to Lucy?"

"She . . . she ran away!" Ben said in a shaky voice.

Bobby jumped up. "Ran away? Where?"

"That way." Ben was confused. He pointed in one direction. "Or maybe that way." He pointed in the other direction.

"Which way was it?" Shawn demanded.

"I'm not sure." Ben was almost crying. "But she was chasing a big orange C-A-T!"